NIGHT AT THE MUSEUM™
BATTLE OF THE SMITHSONIAN

A Capital Adventure

Library of Congress catalog card number: 2008940710
ISBN 978-0-06-171556-3

Book design by Sean Boggs
❖
First Edition

NIGHT AT THE MUSEUM™
BATTLE OF THE SMITHSONIAN

A Capital Adventure

Adapted by Jasmine Jones
Based on the screenplay by
Robert Ben Garant & Thomas Lennon

HarperEntertainment
An Imprint of HarperCollinsPublishers

THE
MUSEUM OF
NATURAL
HISTORY

CHAPTER
1

"Big news, Larry," Ed said, as he trotted after his boss. "We got the big chain meeting."

Larry Daley didn't break his stride. "When?"

"Three days."

"Okay, okay." Larry marched through the gleaming offices of Daley Devices. Larry used to be a Night Guard at the Museum of Natural History in New York City. He had discovered that the museum had a magic Egyptian tablet. The tablet made things come alive at night. Larry had invented a lot of things to help keep the exhibits—like the naughty capuchin monkey, the playful T. rex skeleton, and the cavemen—from getting out of control. The inventions had made Larry rich, and he had quit his Night Guard job. Now he owned his own company. "We've got a lot of work to do. We're going to be working right through until we're sitting at that table."

Ed nodded. He knew that the big chain meeting was very important. It would make the company a lot of money.

Larry climbed into his limousine. "To the museum, Mr. Daley?" his driver asked. "It's the first of the month."

"Right, that's today." Larry finished writing a text message. The limo pulled up to the museum. Larry hurried up the steps. Ignoring the closed sign, he walked into the marble entranceway; he was paying his monthly visit to his friends.

The museum director, Dr. McPhee, hurried out of his office. "Excuse me, civilian, do you not know how to read? The museum is closed for—"

McPhee stopped when he recognized Larry. "Why, if it isn't our very own Mr. Success Story, Mr. 'I'm Too Good for Eleven-Fifty an Hour.' Haven't seen you in a few months."

"Yeah, I've been busy." Larry looked around. The lobby was crowded with crates and boxes. Stainless-steel disks were tucked into every corner of the lobby. "What's going on here?"

"Progress, Mr. Daley," McPhee said. "The future." He showed Larry how the new hologram technology worked. A talking Theodore Roosevelt greeted Larry.

Larry nodded. "So, you guys are, like, adding some new interactive exhibits."

"They'll be replacing the old exhibits," McPhee explained.

Larry's heart thudded. *Replacing the exhibits?* he thought. But they were his friends! "What? Where are the old ones going?"

"Deep storage. In the Federal Archives. At the Smithsonian."

That's in Washington, D.C.! Larry thought. He said, "There's got to be something we can do."

"Oh, I know! We can arrange a Save the Wax Animals benefit!" McPhee said sarcastically. "They leave in the morning. Cheerio." He tossed his scarf over his shoulder and strode toward the exit just as the sun set.

Something hard nuzzled Larry's cheek. It was an enormous Tyrannosaurus rex skeleton. "Hey, boy. Yeah, good

to see you, too, pal. How you doing? You doing okay with all this?" Larry motioned to the crates, but Rexy was busy sniffing at a bag that Larry had brought. He always liked to bring the T. rex a treat. "What, you think I got something in here for you?" Larry asked innocently. Rexy yanked a large pull toy out of the bag. Actually, it was several pull toys tied together. Larry grabbed the other end. "You think you're stronger than me? Yeah, I don't think so . . ." Larry and Rexy played tug-of-war. Rexy got excited. He shook his head hard. Larry flew through the air and landed among the crates.

Pop! Pop! Pop! The lids on the crates spouted open, like fountains. The exhibits climbed out.

"Lawrence," Theodore Roosevelt called, as he rode up on his horse, "good to see you, lad."

"Yeah, you too, Teddy. Look, McPhee just told me what's going on around here. I had no idea."

"Hey!" cried a voice. "Want to lend a hand over here?" An arm the size of a small French fry was sticking out of a hole in the crate. Larry opened the lid. His friend, the tiny cowboy, Jedidiah, climbed out.

"Oh, hey, Jed. How are you doing?" Larry asked.

"Well, lookee here!" Jed crowed. "Mr. Big-in-the-Britches himself! Come by just in time to see us off."

"Yeah, Jed, I heard. . . . I don't even know how this happened."

◈ 9 ◈

"You weren't here, Gigantor!" Jed cried. "That's how it happened. Fact is, there's no one else to speak for us during business hours."

The giant stone head from Easter Island chimed in. "None none, dum-dum."

"Look, guys, maybe it won't be so bad." Larry tried to sound cheerful. "We're talking about the Smithsonian here. It's like the Hall of Fame of museums."

"That ain't the point, Gigantor!" Jed shook his head. "The point is we're being shipped out! This Smithsonian could be Shangri-doodle-la, but it ain't never gonna be home!"

Larry stood there, wishing there were something he could do.

"Come now!" Teddy scolded Jed. "Lawrence, forgive them. It's an emotional time for all of us. It's also our last night as a family. So who'll join me for one last stroll within these hallowed halls? My dear?" He reached out to Sacajawea, the famous Native American tracker. "Shall we?" He helped her onto his horse.

Slowly and sadly, the friends moved through the halls of the museum. They all wanted to say good-bye to their home.

Larry stayed at the museum all night. As sunrise approached, the displays climbed back into their crates.

"Travel safe, my love," Teddy told Sacajawea. He kissed her on the cheek.

Larry noticed the naughty capuchin monkey, Dexter, arranging the straw in his crate. "Hey, Dex," Larry said. "You want some help there?"

But the monkey just jumped into his crate and slammed the lid closed.

Larry looked around. "Where's your crate, Teddy?" he asked. The president had returned to his pedestal.

"I won't be making this journey, Lawrence. It seems I, Rexy, and a few other signature items will be staying, for now."

"Without the tablet?" Larry asked.

Teddy glanced around sharply. He leaned close to Larry. "Well, Lawrence," he whispered, "in truth, Ahkmenrah's tablet will be staying with him upstairs."

"What?" Larry's heart sank. Without the tablet, his friends couldn't come alive. Larry stared at the crates. He was sure that his friends didn't know the truth. Sacajawea waved sadly before shutting the lid on her crate. "Are you going to be okay?" Larry asked.

Teddy sighed. "I shall do my best. And who knows? Sometimes, the greatest change carries with it even greater opportunity. Look at you, Lawrence. You left this place and made quite a life for yourself."

"Yeah," Larry said slowly, "I guess so."

Suddenly, his meeting with the big chain didn't seem very important.

CHAPTER
2

"**S**o they're gone?" Larry's son, Nick, put a bag full of Chinese food containers on the table. "There's nothing you could do?"

"I wish there were." Larry shook his head sadly. "I spoke to McPhee. I called the board of directors, but the displays shipped out this morning."

Nick eyed the containers of food that his father was unpacking. "Dad, this is a lot of food."

"Yeah, uh, Ed from work is going to be joining us later on," Larry admitted.

"You're working tonight," Nick said. It wasn't really a question. His father had been working a lot of nights lately.

"What's the big deal, buddy?" Larry's voice was cheerful, but it seemed kind of fake to Nick. "I used to work every night, right?"

Nick thought about that for a moment. "That was different. That was when you had, like, the coolest job in the world."

"Well, cool doesn't pay for your school, this apartment, or that MP3 player you're using. Besides, my job's just a different kind of cool." The phone rang, and Larry pressed the speaker button. "Larry Daley."

"Gigantor! It's me, Jed!" Jedidiah's voice rang through the apartment. He sounded like he was in trouble. "The monkey stole the tablet, and now we're in a world o' hurt! Kahmunrah—he's Ahkmenrah's big brother—he's here, and trust me, not a friendly! I don't know how much longer we can fight 'em off!"

"Calla foota!" Larry knew that voice—it was Attila, shouting at his Huns to attack!

Suddenly, the line went dead.

Larry turned to his son. "Grab your jacket. I'm dropping you off at Mom's."

Ed was just getting off the elevator as they stepped into the hallway. "Larry! Hey, where you going?" he asked.

"Something's come up. I've got to head out of town." Larry didn't have time to explain the whole situation—not that he could have, anyway. All he knew was that Dexter had stolen the tablet and that things at the Smithsonian had gotten out of control! Larry steered Nick toward the elevator.

◈ 14 ◈

Ed blocked Larry's path. "Wait, wait. Just hold on a second. You do understand, the big chain meeting is the day after tomorrow. This is the one we've been waiting for."

"And I'll be there, Ed," Larry promised. He pushed his way past Ed. "But right now, I've got to go."

"Where are you going?" Ed cried.

Larry punched the button for the first floor. "Washington," he said, as the elevator doors closed.

CHAPTER
3

Larry stepped out of the cab and hurried up the steps to the Smithsonian National Air and Space Museum. Larry slowed down as he walked inside. His heart sank. *This place is enormous,* he realized. *How will I ever find my friends?*

A tour guide was standing nearby, speaking to a group of tourists. "Welcome to the biggest museum in the world," the guide said. "In fact, the Smithsonian is comprised of nineteen different museums. The Air and Space museum is just one of them."

"Uh, hi, excuse me?" Larry said to the tour guide. "Can you tell me how to get into the Federal Archives?"

"Um, sure. Be a historical document worthy of storing for all eternity," the tour guide joked. "I'm kidding. The archives are underground in a secure area.

They're not open to the public. It's too bad, too, because I saw them once and, gang, it's a trip."

The tour moved on. Larry headed in the other direction. He checked out some of the displays. He saw a monkey in a space suit, dozens of airplanes, a display of the moon landing, and even a group of Albert Einstein paperweights in the gift shop. But he couldn't find a way to get downstairs.

He went to the National Gallery of Art. Then he crossed the National Mall and headed toward the Smithsonian Castle. The Castle is an old brick building that looks like a palace in a fairy tale. Larry stepped inside and saw a display of American gangsters. Nearby was a collection of artifacts. An ancient gate was at the center.

The Gate of Kahmunrah, read the sign. *Mythic door to the underworld.*

"Kahmunrah," Larry whispered. It was the name that Jed had mentioned over the phone.

There was a large notch in the door. It was exactly the same size and shape as the tablet. Larry stepped forward to get a better look.

"Hey!" A guard hurried over, hollering. "No touching. It looks to me like you were moving in with ITT—Intent to Touch."

"There was no intent," Larry insisted, "to touch."

The guard narrowed his eyes. "Because if you want to, go right ahead. Touch it. I stand around all day, just waiting for some punk like you to come along and make my shift interesting."

Larry frowned at the scruffy-looking guard. In Larry's opinion, this kid looked too young to be trusted guarding ancient treasures. "Are you threatening me"—he read the guard's name tag—"Brandon?"

Brandon sneered. He pulled open his jacket to reveal a large, heavy flashlight. "I don't know, am I?"

Larry reached out. Very delicately, he touched Kahmunrah's gate.

"I knew you were a toucher!" Brandon shrieked. He lunged at Larry. But Larry spun away. He wrapped Brandon

in a tight grip and took away his flashlight. "Brandon, seriously, you don't know who you're dealing with here," Larry growled. "You think you know what it means to be a museum guard? I've seen things you can't *imagine*. I'm gonna let you go, and we're going to go our separate ways, understood?"

Larry let him go. But he had taken Brandon's card key. He hurried down a corridor and made his way down a hallway marked "Employees Only."

He dialed Nick on his mobile phone. "I'm in. Now, talk me into the Archives."

Larry told Nick where he was. Nick found a map of the

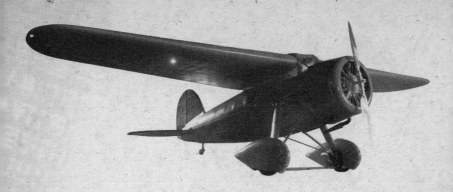

Smithsonian on the Internet. "Okay, turn right—there should be a stairwell coming up on your left," Nick said. "It's kind of a maze down there. Those underground tunnels connect a bunch of different buildings. It could get complicated. . . ."

"Yeah, well, we better move fast, because sundown's in"—Larry checked his watch—"twenty-eight minutes."

"When you get down to B level, you're gonna want to take a—" Nick's voice disappeared.

Larry looked down at his phone. He had no reception! He wandered around underground for a while. Larry felt the seconds ticking away on his watch.

Finally, he made his way into a secure area. It was dark, and Larry had to turn on his flashlight. "Where are you guys?" he muttered.

Larry came across a crate. He pulled back the canvas cover. Long, rubber tentacles tumbled out. It was a giant squid! Larry slammed the lid and latched it.

Larry made his way into the conservation area. He saw a miniature of Octavius, the great general; a horse belonging to General Custer; and a figure of Amelia Earhart, the first female pilot to fly solo across the Atlantic Ocean. Larry swung his flashlight beam. He gasped as it landed on a battle scene. The giant cargo crate from the Museum of Natural History was completely surrounded by Egyptian warriors. A fierce-looking pharaoh stood at the front of the troops. All of the figures were frozen.

Nearby, a familiar monkey stood on a high crate. He was holding the tablet of Ahkmenrah. It was Dexter. "Troublemaker," Larry said to the frozen monkey. "We're going to talk about this later."

Just then, the tablet started to glow. Larry reached for it.

But things had already started coming to life.

The pharaoh shouted at his warriors. They shut the crate and locked it. Then the pharaoh turned to Larry. "The tablet, if you please."

Larry pretended that he wasn't frightened. "I'm sorry, who are you?"

"I am Kahmunrah," the pharaoh said. "Great king of the great kings, and from the darkest depths of ancient history, I have *come to life!*"

"No need to yell," Larry told him. "I mean, no offense, I know it's a big deal for you, coming to life and all. Less of a big deal for me."

"Who are you?" Kahmunrah asked.

"Larry Daley, Daley Devices. Actually, I'm kind of tight with your brother back in the city. Ahkmenrah. Good kid."

Kahmunrah's expression turned angry. "Oh, yes, my baby brother, the favorite son. Mother always gave him everything he wanted . . . including the throne that was rightfully mine! Well, now begins the era of Kahmunrah. Give me the tablet."

"Don't give it to him, Gigantor!" cried a voice from the crate. It was Jed.

Larry tightened his grip on the tablet.

"Silence, miniature!" the pharaoh cried. "My brother was always too weak to embrace the tablet's full power. With it, I shall finally unlock the Gate to the Underworld and bring my army from the Land of the Dead, where they have been

waiting these three thousand years. So, if you would be so kind, hand it over."

"Oh. All you want is the tablet?" Larry asked innocently. "I thought you'd want . . . the cube. If all you want is the tablet, here you go. Have a good day in the underworld." He handed over the tablet as if it were no big deal.

"What is this cube?" Kahmunrah asked.

"You know, the cube that turns all who oppose you to dust?" Larry acted like everyone knew about the cube. "But that's cool. I know your brother didn't want to mess with it, either."

"I am not my brother," Kahmunrah insisted. "Take me to the cube!"

Larry led the way. "Row B, eight-dash-forty-two," he said, as he arrived at a large crate. "Have at it."

"With the tablet of Ahkmenrah and this cube, my power will know no bounds!" He pointed to Larry. "Now open it!"

Larry was very nervous as he walked toward the crate. He flipped open the clasp. He jumped out of the way as the box slammed open and two huge tentacles spilled out! The giant squid rose up. It grabbed a warrior and then lashed out at Kahmunrah. The tablet flew out of his hand. Larry raced after it.

"I still have your friends!" Kahmunrah shouted after Larry. Then he turned to his warriors. "Get me that tablet!"

They ran after Larry. He dashed down hallways and around corners. Finally, he turned down a hall. The squid

◆ 24 ◆

was blocking the way. When he turned back, he saw the Egyptians. Larry was cornered. But suddenly, a motorcycle zoomed into view. General Custer was driving it! He skidded to a stop in front of Larry.

"Take the wheel!" Custer shouted, as he climbed into the sidecar. "I'll handle the rest!"

"What's the plan?" Larry asked, as they took off.

"Who needs a plan?" Custer demanded, as he drove straight toward the Egyptians. "We're Americans! We don't plan—we *do*! Hang on!" The Egyptians flew backward like bowling pins. The motorcycle rounded a corner. "See that? Act first, think later! You're in good hands—General George A. Custer of the Fighting U.S. Seventh Cavalry. Yee-haw!" He stood up in the sidecar. *Bam!* He hit a low shelf and was knocked off the motorcycle. "I'm all right!" Custer called, as he struggled to his feet. "Keep going, friend!"

But when Larry turned a corner, he had to screech to a stop. A woman was standing in his path! "What's the rumpus, Ace?" she asked.

"Listen, lady, I can't really stop right—"

"*Lady?* The name is Amelia. Amelia Earhart? You may have heard of me. I'm not one to shy away from danger."

Larry jumped off the motorcycle. "How about spears?" he asked, as the Egyptians ran toward them. "Are you one to shy away from spears?"

"Let's ankle, Skipper." Amelia dragged Larry toward the stairwell. "What do these gentlemen downstairs want with you, anyway?"

"They want this." Larry held up the tablet. "And I can't let them have it."

"So why don't you just take it and skedaddle?" Amelia asked.

"My friends are being held down there, and I've got to get them," Larry explained.

"Well, then, let's hightail it, Cappie," Amelia said.

CHAPTER
4

"I am Kahmunrah, half god once removed on my mother's side. Ruler of Egypt, future ruler of— everything else. I'm in need of some new generals to join me in my plan to conquer this world. I have studied your placards, and I have selected you. Al Capone, Napoleon Bonaparte, Ivan the Terrible, you are some of the most evil, feared leaders in history. Gentlemen, really, really fantastic to meet you." Kahmunrah smiled at the villains. "So, are you with me, gentlemen?"

"Yeah, sure," Al Capone said. Napoleon and Ivan the Terrible said yes, too. Their men stood behind them, ready for orders.

"Superb." Kahmunrah grinned. "Then bring Larry Daley of Daley Devices and the Golden Tablet to me!"

"All right, troops," Custer said. Al Capone's thugs had captured him and put him in the crate with Larry's friends. Now the thugs were guarding the crate. Inside, Custer was announcing his escape plan. "Here's what we're going to do. On the third bugle blast, I shall loudly announce attack! At which point we shall dive out of this box and attack. What do you think?"

"I know I'm just a tracker and you're a general, but won't yelling 'attack' alert them that we're about to attack?" Sacajawea asked.

"Excuse me! Coming through!" A tiny figure struggled through a small hole in the crate. "Happy to help!"

"Who are you?" Custer asked.

"Octavius, Roman commander, greatest military tactician of all time."

"If you're such a great commander, Octavius, what's your battle plan?" Custer asked.

"Simple. All we require to defeat our sworn adversary are three to four hundred elephants," Octavius said.

Custer frowned. "I think my 'attack on the word *attack*' plan is superior. So that's what we're going to do."

But Octavius wasn't ready to give in. "I vow to aid your campaign. I assure you, we are simply a few elephants short of victory."

"Wake up, feather hat," Jed snapped. "There ain't no elephant or elephantlike beast within a thousand miles of here. Now my gigantic buddy's out there trying to save us, and the least I can do is pitch in. You do what you're going to do. As for me, I need to escape." Jed headed for the hole that Octavius had come in through.

He knew it was time for action.

Larry and Amelia were hiding in the rotunda. Napoleon's troops were nearby.

"Is it just me," Amelia asked, "or is there music in the air?"

Larry looked up. Three cupids were flying above them. One was playing a lyre, and the other two were singing. "Hey, guys . . . baby angels . . . could you stop that?" Larry whispered. "We're trying to hide!"

The soldiers looked over. They headed toward the rotunda.

Larry and Amelia ducked away. But they came face to face with . . . a giant hat. Below the hat was Napoleon Bonaparte. "You are now my prisoner, *s'il vous plaît*," Napoleon said. "Now zis way, or you die."

He led Larry away.

CHAPTER
5

"Hey, boss." One of Al Capone's thugs held out a birdcage. Jed was sitting on a birdie swing inside. "We found this one trying to escape."

Kahmunrah peered at Jed. "You're in luck, tiny cowboy. You're just in time to see me take my rightful place as ruler of all the gods' domain."

Just then, Napoleon and his men walked in with Larry. Kahmunrah reached for the tablet. "Now, after three thousand years, my evil army shall be unleashed!"

Nothing happened.

"*Ahem.* I said, my evil army shall be . . . unleashed!"

More nothing.

"Mother and Father must have changed the combination," Kahmunrah said.

Ivan the Terrible pointed to the hieroglyphics on the

tablet. "Perhaps they left some kind of clue."

Kahmunrah glowered at Larry. "What are you smiling about?"

Larry shrugged. "Nothing. Sorry this whole unleashing-the-underworld thing didn't work out for you. Anyway, in a couple hours you'll just be frozen in some angry position, and I'll take my buddies out of here, and that'll be that. I got all night."

Kahmunrah narrowed his eyes dangerously. He plucked Jed out of the birdcage. "Well, *he* doesn't," Kahmunrah said. He put Jed in an hourglass. Sand spilled down on Jed. "From the looks of this, I'd say he has a little over an hour. You know this tablet. You may not know the combination, but I'm giving you an hour to figure it out. If you don't, I kill your friends."

Jed looked at Larry. "You got this partner," Jed said. "I know you do."

Larry hurried away. He had to find the combination!

Larry ran into Amelia in the art gallery.

"I've got to get this tablet translated right now," Larry told her.

"Hello?" called a voice. "Some assistance here?"

Larry spotted a bust of Theodore Roosevelt. "Teddy!" he cried. "Perfect. I really need you to translate what's written on this tablet. Do you read hieroglyphics?"

"Of course," said the statue. "Oh, yes. This is a simple one. Bird . . . man with spear . . . sideways fish . . . beetle . . . vase."

"So what does it mean?" Amelia asked.

"It means a man with a spear is trying to trap a bird and a sideways fish in a vase," Teddy said. "Also, there's a beetle."

Larry frowned. "I don't think that's what it actually means."

Teddy looked at the tablet again. "Another possible translation is: You will find the combination you seek . . . if you figure out the secret . . . at the heart of the pharaoh's tomb."

"Okay, so what does *that* mean?" Larry asked.

"I don't know," Teddy admitted.

Larry knew that he needed someone really smart to help him with the tablet. Suddenly, he had an idea. "I saw a bunch of Einsteins," he told Amelia.

They ran toward the Air and Space Museum. They didn't realize that Kahmunrah was watching them. "He's trying to escape with the tablet!" Kahmunrah cried, gazing out the window. "Ivan! Send your men to stop them!"

Ivan the Terrible's men raced to stop Larry and Amelia. They blocked the path to the Air and Space Museum. Larry and Amelia saw the men's lanterns in the darkness.

"Criminy!" Amelia cried.

"Follow me." Larry led her up the steps to the Lincoln Memorial. "We should be okay hiding in here for a while."

The enormous sculpture of Abraham Lincoln towered above them. For a few moments, everything was silent.

Then someone yawned—loudly. "Now," said a booming voice, "where the devil did I put my hat?" The giant sculpture of Lincoln looked around and then stood up.

"No, no, no!" Larry cried. He tried to stop Lincoln from walking out of the memorial. "I can't let you go out there! This is really going to freak a lot of people out."

"Mr. President, will you please sit down?" Amelia asked politely.

"I am doing it for you, miss." Lincoln sat back in his chair just as Ivan's men marched past.

"Thank you," Amelia said. Then she and Larry hurried off to the Air and Space Museum. Amelia found a bunch of Einsteins at the information desk. They were paperweights. Each was lying on his stomach, scribbling equations.

"Mr. Einsteins?" Larry said. They all looked up.

"Gentlemen," Amelia said, "we're trying to crack the combination to this

36

doodad." She pointed to the tablet. "The writing here says we'll find it if we figure out the secret at the heart of the pharaoh's tomb."

One of the Einsteins laughed. "It's a riddle! The answer's in the question. *Figure out the secret at the heart of the pharaoh's tomb!*"

"*Saying it with emphasis on every word doesn't help me!*" Larry griped.

"Figure," the Einstein repeated. "It's a figure—i.e., a number!"

"And pharaoh's tomb," another Einstein piped up, "i.e., the pyramids."

"Don't you get it, kid?" The first Einstein laughed again. "You're looking for the secret number at the heart of the pyramids."

A broad grin spread across Amelia's face. "The answer's *pi*!"

For a moment, Larry thought she said "pie." He shook his head, confused. *What does dessert have to do with anything?* he wondered.

"Three-point-one-four," Amelia explained. "*Pi* is the name of a number."

"Three-point-one-four-one-five-nine-two-six-five, to be exact," Einstein corrected. "The Egyptians knew all about pi."

"Wow," Larry said. "Thanks. Okay, three-point-one-four . . . two . . ."

"No, three-point-one-four-one-five-nine-two-six-five," Einstein said.

Larry tried to remember the number. "Three-point-one-four-one-five-nine-two-six . . ."

"I've got it," Amelia told him. "So what's our next move, partner?"

She and Larry were already walking toward the exit.

"We've got about seven minutes to get out of here and get back to Jed," Larry said.

"How do you expect for us to get over there in time?" Amelia asked.

Larry started toward the exhibit of the moon landing. "I was thinking we'd take the moon rover." He pointed to the space buggy that the astronauts used to explore the surface of the moon.

"I've got a better idea," Amelia said with a smile. After all, her very own plane was nearby in a museum display.

"No, I think the rover's pretty much the way to go." Larry kept walking toward the buggy.

Amelia stepped in his way. "You're afraid to fly, aren't you?"

"No, I'm just afraid to fly . . . with you."

"Me? I'm one of the most famous pilots in the history of aviation."

"Yeah, famous for *getting lost*," Larry shot back.

Amelia looked shocked. After all, she had crossed the

Atlantic Ocean *alone*. She had flown across the United States in an old-fashioned gyroplane! She was an *amazing* pilot. But Larry thought of her as someone who got lost? She couldn't believe it.

"I'm sorry," Larry said, "but it's true." He tried to move past her, but Amelia blocked his path.

"Mr. Daley, I assure you that I have never been lost a day in my life," Amelia said. "I may not have always been on course. But I was always where I belonged. In that cockpit, with blue sky all around. Doing what I loved." She looked into his eyes. "It seems to me, Mr. Daley, that if anyone here's gotten 'lost,' it's you."

Larry thought about that. He realized that he'd actually been having fun on this crazy adventure with Amelia. In fact, Larry hadn't had this much fun in years.

Not since he left his job as a museum guard.

It was as if a lightbulb had gone off over his head.

Ding!

Amelia and Larry turned their heads. An elevator door had just opened. Al Capone, Napoleon, and Ivan the Terrible spilled out—followed by their men!

"No time for your rover now, Mr. Daley!" Amelia cried. She raced up the stairs. Larry was right behind her.

They raced along the upper level. Amelia looked up. "It'll have to do," she said.

◆ 39 ◆

Larry followed her gaze. "No," he said, when he saw the plane she was looking at. It was the first working plane ever made—the Wright brothers' 1903 flyer. It was hanging from the ceiling. "It's made out of balsa wood and cloth!" Larry cried.

But Amelia just climbed aboard. "Hop on, slowpoke!"

The bad guys raced up the stairs. A group of African-American pilots blocked their way. It was the Tuskegee Airmen, heroes of World War II.

Larry had just enough time to climb over the railing and hop onto the plane. The plane was meant for only one person. Larry and Amelia had to lie on their stomachs in the cockpit. The engine revved. The propellers spun. The plane strained against the cables.

Snap! Snap! Snap!

The plane broke free. Amelia piloted it down the hall.

"Thanks, fellas!" Amelia waved to the Tuskegee Airmen.

The plane zoomed through a large doorway. Larry and Amelia soared over the National Mall and past the Capitol dome. They flew past the Washington Monument.

They were on their way.

CHAPTER 6

"You look nervous, ramen noodle," Jed said to Kahmunrah. "Giving up yet?"

The pharaoh glared at him. He picked up the hourglass and shook it. Sand poured down on the tiny cowboy. "Let's see if we can make time fly. . . ."

Just then, there was a loud crash. The stained glass ceiling shattered as the Wright flyer burst through. Kahmunrah dropped the hourglass and dived for cover.

Larry leaped off the plane while it was still moving. It came to a stop at the end of the room. Amelia was still inside.

Larry grabbed the hourglass and flipped it over.

"Thank you, partner," Jed said.

"Anytime, buddy," Larry told him. He turned to Kahmunrah. "Open the crate and release my friends, and

42

I'll give you the combination."

"We already got the combination," Al Capone announced. He walked in, followed by the rest of Kahmunrah's goons. Capone was holding a tiny Einstein. "It's pi."

"I'm sorry, Larry," Einstein said.

The bad guys surrounded Larry. One grabbed the tablet. Kahmunrah placed it in the gate's notch. The tablet fit perfectly. Kahmunrah pressed the numbers: 314159265. The tablet started to glow and hum. Thunder shook the museum. The tablet flashed, filling the room with light. The door in the gate groaned open. It led to darkness. Strange, ghostly horns sounded.

Soldiers began to march in through the door. But they weren't men. They were Horus-like soldiers: Their bodies were human, but they had fierce hawk-heads. They wore golden armor.

"Horuses," Kahmunrah said. "My warriors, send Larry Daley and his friends to their doom."

The Horuses raised their spears and marched toward Larry.

"Hold!" cried a voice.

Everyone turned. There was something in the doorway. It was . . .

Well, it was small.

"The mighty Octavius has returned!" shouted the

miniature. He rode into the room on the back of a squirrel. "You were correct, sweet-tempered and gentle Jedidiah. It is a challenge, indeed, to find a wild elephant in this empire. But I refused to come back having failed you." He galloped toward Kahmunrah. "Do you wish to surrender honorably?"

"This is your big rescue?" Kahmunrah demanded.

The squirrel galloped up to the pharaoh. "No," Octavius announced. "This is."

Crash!

Glass shattered from the ceiling. Everyone looked up.

Abraham Lincoln towered over them. It was the marble giant from the Lincoln Memorial.

"I brought help," Octavius said, "as I swore I would."

Kahmunrah looked at his Horus soldiers. They were frozen in place. "What are you waiting for?" he screeched. "Attack it!"

The Horuses threw their spears. *Clink, clink, clink!* The spears bounced off Lincoln's marble chest. The stone president grabbed a few of the soldiers and tossed them aside.

The rest of the Horuses raced back through the gate. They slammed it shut behind them.

Kahmunrah stared at the gate. "Well," he said, "that's just . . . fabulous."

Lincoln looked down at Larry. "It appears my work here is done," he said with a smile. The giant statue turned to go.

"Wait, what?" Larry cried. "You're leaving?"

"Your small Roman friend brought me here to even things up," Lincoln explained. "I believe that now to be the case."

"No, that's not the case," Larry said. "We are still very, very outnumbered." It was just him, Jed, Octavius, and a squirrel against Kahmunrah and all of his bad guys!

"Not anymore," Lincoln said. He pointed toward the hall. A bugle sounded.

Amelia was there. She was with General Custer and the rest of Larry's friends from New York. They had found help in the rest of the museum, too.

"You'll be fine now," Lincoln told Larry. "Just remember my most famous words."

Larry nodded. "A house divided cannot stand!"

Lincoln walked away, back toward his memorial.

Custer led the charge.

"Don't just stand there!" Kahmunrah shouted. "Get them!"

A Russian soldier swung a club at Larry. It missed Larry, but Jed's hourglass went flying. It landed upright, and sand began to flow over Jed again.

The armies met with a crash. Napoleon, Al Capone, and Ivan the Terrible commanded their men. Sacajawea used her arrows, the giant squid used its tentacles, and some of the statues fought with iron and marble fists. It was a fierce battle.

Larry saw that the tablet was still in the gate. He motioned to Amelia. They both made their way toward it. The battle raged around them.

Octavius ran across the floor. He had to get to Jed before the sand buried him!

"You hear that?" Octavius cried to him. "They need us!"

"Sorry, but I think this here cowboy's seen his last hoedown," Jed said dramatically.

Octavius took off his helmet. "No need for final words," he said. Then he smashed his helmet against the hourglass. The glass shattered, and the sand came flooding out.

Octavius helped Jed to his feet.

"Thank you," Jed said, "friend."

Octavius smiled. He put on his helmet. Jed put on his hat.

"Let's get to work," Jed said.

They raced through the battle, stabbing the bad guys' ankles.

Larry reached the gate. He grabbed the tablet and handed it to Amelia. "I need you to keep this safe. No matter what happens to me, keep it safe."

They ducked behind the gate.

"I take it you have a plan?" Amelia asked.

"Time to divide the house," Larry said. He stepped to the front of the gate.

Ivan the Terrible, Napoleon, and Capone were waiting for him.

"The tablet," Ivan demanded. "Now."

Larry looked around. "Okay," he said slowly. "You guys win. Just tell me who's in charge and I'll hand it over. Or I could just give it to Kahmunrah—you know, your master."

The villains looked at one another.

"*Nyet!*" Ivan said. "He is not our master."

"He's not?" Larry shrugged. "Okay, which one of you is the boss?"

All three reached for the tablet.

Ivan slapped Capone's hand away. "This man is a peasant!" Ivan shouted. "I am the only one among us of noble blood!"

"Yeah," Larry agreed, "but Napoleon does have more medals and a bigger hat."

Capone slapped Napoleon's hands away. "You may have medals, but if you put your little hands on that tablet, it'll be the last thing those teeny mitts ever touch!"

Napoleon slapped Capone's hands. Capone lunged at him. Napoleon fell backward, into Ivan. Soon, all three were smacking one another.

Larry started to back away. But he backed right into Kahmunrah. The pharaoh had a sword.

"Very clever," Kahmunrah growled. "Get them to fight amongst themselves. At least now I'll have the pleasure of killing you myself!" He raised his sword.

Clang!

The sword hit metal. Sparks rained down. Larry had his flashlight, and he knew how to use it.

Amelia appeared at the gate. She put the tablet in its slot. She pressed the combination. The door opened.

Larry fought hard. He backed Kahmunrah toward the

door. Larry knocked the sword away with a lightning-fast move.

Kahmunrah gaped. "What are you?" he whispered.

"I'm the Night Guard," Larry said. Then he pushed him through the door.

"No!" Kahmunrah shouted.

Larry pulled the door shut. Now Kahmunrah could spend some time with his Horus warriors. A long time. Larry pulled the tablet out of its slot.

Amelia smiled at him. "If I didn't know better, Mr. Daley, I'd say someone's found their moxie."

Larry nodded. He'd found his moxie, all right. And so had his friends. Kahmunrah, Ivan the Terrible, Napoleon, and Al Capone had all been defeated. Just in the nick of time.

Larry looked at his watch.

◆ 51 ◆

"Oh, man—sunrise is in an hour. I've got to get you all back to the museum."

"But they don't want us there anymore, Gigantor," Jed said.

"Well, I do," Larry said. "Miss Earhart, think you could hook us up with a ride?"

Amelia grinned. "With pleasure, of course."

She raced back to the Air and Space Museum and got her plane. Then she loaded everyone onto it. Then they waved good-bye to their friends from the Smithsonian as they soared toward New York.

CHAPTER
7

Amelia's plane touched down right in front of the Museum of Natural History. "Okay," Larry said, as his friends deplaned, "everybody out. Remember to stay with your buddy."

He handed the tablet to the capuchin monkey. "Dex, give this back to Ahkmenrah. I think you owe him an apology. Sac, get everybody down to the basement."

Sacajawea nodded.

"Well," Amelia said to Larry, "you're back where you belong."

Larry looked up at the museum. "Yeah," he said, "I think so."

They were silent for a moment. "I guess I should be going," Amelia said at last.

Larry looked at his friend. He knew that she would

be just a wax statue again in a short while. But he didn't know how to tell her. "Look, Amelia, come morning—"

"I know what's coming, Mr. Daley," Amelia told him. "I've known all along. But it doesn't matter. You've given me the adventure of a lifetime in one night. And I have a feeling it's going to be a beautiful sunrise." She leaned toward him. "Have fun," she whispered.

"Amelia," Larry said. "Good-bye."

Amelia climbed into the cockpit. She gave Larry a thumbs-up. She taxied down the street. Then she took off into the sky.

Jed poked out of one of Larry's pockets. Octavius poked out of the other.

"There she goes," Jed said.

Octavius watched the plane. "Straight toward . . ."

" . . . Canada," Larry said.

Amelia was heading in the wrong direction.

Suddenly, the plane looped around. It headed south, toward Washington, D.C.

Larry walked into the museum lobby. Rexy bounded over. "Hey, boy," Larry said, petting him. He walked past the Easter Island head. "What's up, fathead? How was your night?"

"Not as fun, dum-dum," the head said.

Teddy hugged Sacajawea. He walked over to Larry.

"Thank you for bringing them back," Teddy said. "And while I extend to you a hearty well-done, lad, might I point out that they can't hide in the basement forever."

"I know," Larry said. "I think I've got that figured out."

"Sun come, dum-dum," the Easter Island head said.

Teddy climbed onto his horse. The other displays hurried to the basement. Everyone got into place and waited for the sun to rise.

CHAPTER
8

The sun was just going down over New York City. Larry stepped out the front door of the Museum of Natural History. He was wearing his old guard uniform. A crowd of people on the front stairs was waiting to get inside.

A banner was hanging over the door. *Museum of Natural History*, it read. *Now open late.*

Dr. McPhee walked up to Larry. "Well, well, well," McPhee said. "I see the suit still fits, after these many long years. And what prompted your triumphant return? Not cut out for the corporate jungle, after all?"

Ed was running Larry's company now. Larry was happy for him. Ed really seemed to enjoy the business, much more than Larry ever had. "Yeah, I guess not."

"Well, clearly the world works in mysterious ways,"

McPhee said. "One day we're getting rid of everything old, the next, some rich anonymous donor gives a huge endowment on the condition that everything stay the same."

"That right?" Larry smiled to himself. He knew that the rich donor was himself. He'd spent most of the money he had made from selling the company. It was worth it, though.

"Yes, well, not quite the same," McPhee admitted. He looked around. Everywhere, tour groups were being led by "live" exhibits.

"Bully, lads and ladies!" Teddy cried. "The name's Theodore Roosevelt: naturalist, Rough Rider, and twenty-sixth president of these great United States. Come, lads, the hunt is afoot!" Families hurried after him. Everyone was amazed by the new interactive exhibits.

Well, almost everyone. A group of teenagers looked up at Rexy. The dinosaur skeleton was chewing a bone.

"This place is lame," one of the teenagers griped. "This thing doesn't even look real."

Rexy stood up to his full height. He let out a huge roar.

For a moment, the teens were speechless.

"Whoa," one of them whispered.

McPhee shrugged. "Honestly, today's technology is beyond me."

"Yeah," Larry agreed. "It's . . . something else."

Just then, Larry spotted a woman through the crowd with

an uncanny resemblance to Amelia. Larry walked over to her, but stopped a few steps away, staring.

"Can I . . . help you?" asked the woman.

"Uh, yeah, no, sorry. It's just—you look like someone I . . . know," said Larry.

"Yeah, I get that lot. I have one of those faces," she replied.

"You're not, by any chance, related to Amelia Earhart, are you?" asked Larry, going out on a limb.

"Uh, no. She was that woman who, like, flew across the Pacific, right?" the woman wondered.

"Actually, it was the Atlantic. She was the first woman ever to do it. She was also the first woman to receive the Distinguished Flying Cross and fly across the forty-eight states in a gyroplane," stated Larry.

"Huh. Pretty cool,"

"Yeah . . . she was," Larry said, smiling.

GET REAL!

Abraham Lincoln was a real person.

Did you know...

FACT Lincoln was the tallest president in history. He was 6 feet 4 inches tall.

FACT Lincoln was the first president to wear a beard while in office.

FACT You can see a tiny Abraham Lincoln sitting in the Lincoln Memorial on the back of a penny. (Use a magnifying glass.)

FACT Lincoln is famous! He is portrayed in more movies than any other president.

FACT An eleven-year-old girl suggested that Lincoln would look better with a beard, so he grew one.

FACT Lincoln was the first president born outside of the original thirteen colonies. He was born in Kentucky.

FACT Lincoln had a scar over his right eye. It was from a fight with a gang of thieves!